JUMP ALONG

A FUN BOOK OF MOVEMENT

First published in the U.S. in 1991 by
Carolrhoda Books, Inc.
First published 1990 by Firefly Books Ltd.

Library of Congress Cataloging-in-Publication Data

Morris, Neil.
   Jump along: a fun book of movement/written by Neil Morris;
illustrated by Peter Stevenson.
      p.   cm.—(Fun books of learning)
   "First published in 1990 by Firefly Books Limited...East Sussex
...England"—T.p. verso.
   Summary: A young kangaroo learns from other animals that the only
way he can move around is by jumping.
   ISBN 0-87614-671-X
   [1. Kangaroos—Fiction. 2. Jumping—Fiction.] I. Stevenson,
Peter, 1953-   ill. II. Title. III. Series: Morris, Neil. Fun
books of learning.
PZ7.M8284Ju   1991
[E]—dc20   90-21126
                                                CIP
                                                 AC

Manufactured in Italy by Rotolito Lombarda SpA – Milano

Bound in the United States of America

1 2 3 4 5 6 7 8 9 10 00 99 98 97 96 95 94 93 92 91

JUMP ALONG

A FUN BOOK OF MOVEMENT

by Neil Morris
illustrated by Peter Stevenson

Carolrhoda Books, Inc./Minneapolis

Joe is a shy little kangaroo. He's always hiding in his mother's pouch. While his cousins are jumping around, Joe stays with his mother.

"You're old enough now to jump around on your own," Mom says.
"But I *can't* jump," Joe cries.

"Nonsense!" Joe's father shouts. "All kangaroos can jump."

With that he hops off, and the others follow.

"*I don't want to jump,*" Joe says, closing his eyes.

Now poor Joe is sad.

"I've lost my family because I don't want to jump," he tells the birds.

"Come and fly with us," the birds chirp.

Joe flaps his arms and his tail, but he doesn't take off.

"You can't be in our family if you don't fly," the birds sing as they fly away.

"I'll teach you the best way to get around,"
a snake hisses. "Slither along with me!"

"It feels uncomfortable," Joe tells the snake.

"You look ridiculous!" the snake laughs and
slithers away.

"You could make a good elephant," a loud voice booms. "We stomp all over the place. Would you like to stomp along?"

Joe stamps his feet, but he barely moves.

"I can't stomp so fast," he shouts.

Whatever can I do? Joe wonders.

"We swim around in the water all day," a little fish splutters. "Come in, it's easy!"

Joe wiggles his tail like the fish. But all he does is sink.

"He can't come with us if he can't swim," the fish chant.

"You're scared of water, just like my ducklings!" a mother duck quacks. "Get in line and waddle along with us."

The ducklings don't
like Joe.
"He's not waddling
right," they tell
their mother.

"Waddling will get you nowhere fast," a tiger growls. "Come and prowl with me."

"Am I prowling right?" Joe asks.

But the tiger has prowled off on his own.

"Never trust a tiger!" a little monkey calls. "Climb up to us."

The monkey shows Joe how to climb the tree, but Joe keeps slipping down.

"I can't climb," Joe cries.

"You knocked?" a mole asks. "Come on down. Just burrow!"

Joe tries his best.

"You have to dig much harder," the mole says. "Moles burrow all day and night."

I'll never find a family to get along with, the little kangaroo thinks.

"You wouldn't have liked it down there. It's too dark," a beetle says. "It's better to crawl on top."

Joe begins to hop away.

"But you're not crawling," the beetle complains, "you're hopping!"

"Hopping is fun!" Joe says.

"Not for me," says the beetle, who crawls off.

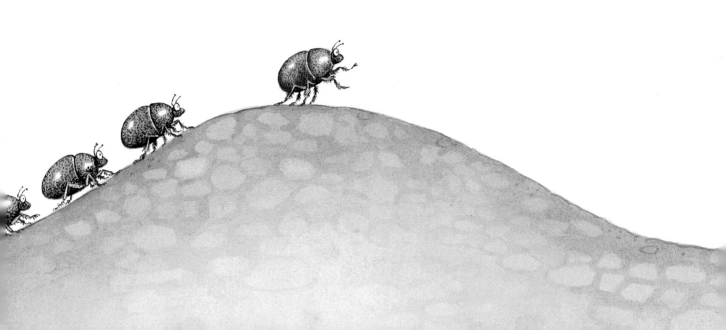

"It's too bad no one else likes leaping," says Joe.

"Well, you could never keep up with me," Frog croaks. "Frogs are the best!"

The little kangaroo jumps farther than the boasting frog.

"I can jump," Joe shouts. "Look at me, I can jump!"

Joe jumps, hops, and leaps along.
"I can jump like a kangaroo!" he cries.

"Of course you can," Joe's father says.
"All kangaroos can jump. Jump along!"